#1

K. Hamel

I am an ARO PUBLISHING
TEN WORD BOOK.

My ten words are:

bump	what
shoe	a
snap	day
squirt	smoke
splash	burnt

Funny Bunny

10 WORDS

Story by Judy Schoder
Pictures by Bob Reese

ISBN 0-89868-069-7 — Library Bound
ISBN 0-89868-080-8 — Soft Bound

Snap!

Shoe.

Snap!

What a day!

What a day!!